# True Adventures and Exciting Sports

商務印書館（香港）有限公司
http://www.commercialpress.com.hk

CENGAGE
Learning™

Australia • Brazil • Japan • Korea • Mexico • Singapore • Spain • United Kingdom • United States

True Adventures and Exciting Sports 挑戰海陸空

Main English text © 2009 Heinle, Cengage Learning
English footnotes © 2009 Heinle, Cengage Learning and The Commercial Press (H.K.) Ltd.
Chinese text © 2009 The Commercial Press (H.K.) Ltd.

香港特別版由Heinle, a part of Cengage Learning 及商務印書館（香港）有限公司聯合出版。
This special Hong Kong edition is co-published by Heinle, a part of Cengage Learning, and The
Commercial Press (H.K.) Ltd.

Director of Content Development:
Anita Raducanu
Series Editor: Rob Waring
Editorial Manager: Bryan Fletcher

Associate Development Editors:
Victoria Forrester, Catherine McCue
責任編輯：黃家麗

出版：

商務印書館（香港）有限公司
香港筲箕灣耀興道3號東匯廣場8樓

Cengage Learning
Units 808-810, 8th floor,
Tins Enterprises Centre,
777 Lai Chi Kok Road, Cheung Sha Wan,
Kowloon, Hong Kong

網址：http://www.commercialpress.com.hk

http://www.cengageasia.com

發行：香港聯合書刊物流有限公司
　　　香港新界大埔汀麗路36號中華商務
　　　印刷大廈3字樓

印刷：中華商務彩色印刷有限公司
版次：2010年3月第1版第2次印刷

ISBN: 978-962-07-1871-7

# 出版説明

本館一向倡導優質閱讀，近年連續推出以 "Q" 為標誌的優質英語學習系列*(Quality English Learning)*，其中《Black Cat 優質英語階梯閱讀》，讀者反應令人鼓舞，先後共推出超過60本。

為進一步推動閱讀，本館引入Cengage 出版之*Footprint Library*，使用*National Geographic*的圖像及語料，編成百科英語階梯閱讀系列，有別於Black Cat 古典文學閱讀，透過現代真實題材，百科英語語境能幫助讀者認識今日的世界各事各物，擴闊視野，提高認識及表達英語的能力。

本系列屬non-fiction (非虛構故事類)讀本，結合閱讀、視像和聽力三種學習功能，是一套三合一多媒介讀本，每本書的英文文章以headwords寫成，headwords 選收自以下數據庫的語料：*Collins Cobuild The Bank of English*、*British National Corpus* 及 *BYU Corpus of American English* 等，並配上精彩照片，另加一張 video/audio 兩用DVD。編排由淺入深，按級提升，只要讀者堅持學習，必能有效提高英語溝通能力。

商務印書館(香港)有限公司

編輯部

# 使用說明

百科英語階梯閱讀分四級，共八本書，是彩色有影有聲書，每本有英語文章供閱讀，根據數據庫如 *Collins Cobuild The Bank of English*、*British National Corpus* 及 *BYU Corpus of American English* 選收常用字詞編寫，配彩色照片及一張video/audio 兩用DVD，結合閱讀、聆聽、視像三種學習方式。

讀者可使用本書：

 學習新詞彙，並透過延伸閱讀(Expansion Reading)練習速讀技巧

 聆聽錄音提高聽力，模仿標準英語讀音

 看短片做練習，以提升綜合理解能力

Grammar Focus解釋語法重點，後附練習題，供讀者即時複習所學，書內其他練習題，有助讀者掌握學習技巧如 scanning, prediction, summarising, identifying the main idea

中英對照生詞表設於書後，既不影響讀者閱讀正文，又具備參考作用

# Contents 目錄

***The CD-ROM contains a video and full recording of the text***

***CD-ROM*** 包括短片和錄音

# Words to Know

This story is set in New Zealand. It happens far from the real capital of Wellington in a place known as the capital, or centre, of adventure – Queenstown.

 **Adventure in the Air.** Read the paragraph and look at the picture. Then match each word or phrase with the correct definition.

In Queenstown, New Zealand, adventure sports are usually fast, fun and sometimes dangerous. Some local people do them as pastimes to have fun in their free time. Visitors often go to Queenstown to do them. Some people go bungee jumping from the bridges over rivers. Other people hike into the mountains, and then fly back in a helicopter.

| | |
|---|---|
| **1.** adventure _____ | **a.** a kind of aircraft that has large turning blades |
| **2.** pastime _____ | **b.** a structure used to cross over something |
| **3.** bungee jumping _____ | **c.** an exciting and dangerous experience |
| **4.** bridge _____ | **d.** take a long walk in a natural area |
| **5.** hike _____ | **e.** an activity done when not working |
| **6.** helicopter _____ | **f.** a sport in which people jump from a high place with a special rope |

river

**B** **Adventure on the Water.** Read the sentences and then complete the paragraph with the underlined words.

Frightening means something makes you afraid.
A jetboat is a kind of boat that goes extremely fast.
A propeller turns around in the water to move a boat.
Shallow describes water which is not deep.
A thrill is a strong feeling of excitement and pleasure.

One popular pastime in Queenstown is riding in a (1)_____.
Some people get a (2)_____ from the speed when they go very fast. This type of boat does not move with a (3)_____, so people can drive it in very little, or (4)_____, water. Driving a jetboat, like bungee jumping, can be a little (5)_____, but some people really like that!

A Jetboat

bungee jumping

helicopter

special rope

New Zealand is a land of many beautiful and quiet natural places, but Queenstown isn't one of them. 'Ahh!' shouts one young man as he speeds towards the earth. Don't worry, he's not **crazy**,[1] he's bungee jumping! You can hear the cries of several more people as they jump from the Nevis High Wire Bungee site.

People come from around the world to do adventure sports in Queenstown – especially bungee jumping. Henry Van Asch works at the jump site. He offers one reason why this site is so popular. 'The **gap**[2] from the **underside**[3] of that little silver **jump pod**[4] out there,' he says as he points to the jump spot, 'is 134 metres, which is about 440 feet.' That's a long way down! The sport must be really fun because there are many people waiting for a chance to do it. What do they feel like before a jump?

---

[1] **crazy:** not having a good mind; not normal
[2] **gap:** a space between two things
[3] **underside:** the bottom surface of sth
[4] **jump pod:** small container supported by metal wire from which people bungee jump

The Nevis High Wire Bungee Site

Most people can hardly wait to go. 'I'm so ready! **Bring it on**!'[1] says one young man as he and his friends wait for their turn. Bungee jumping isn't just for men either; women also enjoy this adventure sport. 'I'm getting excited, actually,' says a young woman who is waiting for her jump time.

As the instructor gets the next person ready, he counts down to the jump: 'Five, four, three, two, one!' The man jumps out of the pod and starts the 134-metre drop to the river. It looks like he's going to hit the ground! Then suddenly he's pulled back up by the special rope, or bungee **cord**,[2] that's connected to his legs. **Phew**![3]

If you like exciting adventure sports, New Zealand is the place to do them. Henry Van Asch explains why he thinks they are so popular. He says that the way of life, or lifestyle, of the people here is very adventurous. 'New Zealand people have a very **immediate lifestyle**[4] a lot of the time,' he says, 'and that's what people can experience when they come here.'

---

[1] **bring it on:** *(slang)* 'let's start'
[2] **cord:** strong thick string
[3] **phew:** used for showing that you are no longer worried about sth
[4] **immediate lifestyle:** *(uncommon use)* here the speaker may mean a risky or adventurous way of living

There's more than just bungee jumping to do in New Zealand. Visitors can also go for a jetboat ride. Riding in a jetboat is a special experience. As one jetboat driver says, 'Ha! [There's] nothing like it!' The jetboat is another one of New Zealand's adventure **inventions**.[1] There's no **propeller**,[2] so the boats can work in shallow water. They can also turn around in a very small space. 'These machines … you can **spin 'em on a dime**!'[3] the jetboat driver says as he turns the boat around quickly.

Jetboats were especially designed to get around New Zealand's shallow rivers, but they're also really good at giving customers a **thrill**.[4] 'Ha ha ha! Yee hee hee!' cries the driver, as he enjoys the speed of the boat. 'This is one of the number-one **pastimes**[5] of people coming to New Zealand … more importantly probably [of people coming to] Queenstown,' he explains when he finally stops for a rest.

---

[1]**invention:** sth new that has never been made before
[2]**propeller:** sth that spins, used for moving a boat
[3]**spin on a dime:** (slang) turn the boats around in a small amount of space
[4]**thrill:** a sudden feeling of being very excited
[5]**pastime:** sth you do for fun in your free time

Jetboat rides are a thrilling adventure sport in New Zealand.

In New Zealand, it seems that nearly every day someone creates another adventure sport. David Kennedy, who is from a company called 'Destination Queenstown', talks about just how many adventure sports there are to do: 'You know, we quite **proudly**[1] call ourselves "The Adventure Capital of the World",' he says. He then adds, 'There are so many adventure activities to do here. In fact, we **worked** it **out**[2] that if you did one of every type of activity, you'd be here for sixty days!'

---

[1]**proud:** pleased or satisfied with a person, object or action
[2]**work sth out:** solve a problem by looking at the facts

One of the newest adventures in Queenstown involves a five-hour hike up a mountain. It's hard work, but fun for everyone. The best part is, at the end of the hike, the hikers don't have to walk all the way down again. How do they get back? A guide for this adventure explains. 'We'll stay here for ten minutes or so … fifteen minutes,' he says, 'then we'll jump in the helicopter and fly back to Queenstown.' The helicopter turns the five-hour hike into a five-minute flight back to the city!

## Scan for Information

**Scan page 12 to find the information.**

1. How long does it take the hikers to get up the mountain?

2. How long do the hikers usually stay at the top of the mountain?

3. How do they travel back to Queenstown after the hike?

4. How long does it take them?

The Kawarau Bridge

All of these different adventure sports really help the tourism industry in New Zealand. They're also part of an adventurous culture that goes back to the **birthplace**[1] of adventure tourism in New Zealand – the Kawarau Bridge. The bridge was the world's first **commercial**[2] bungee-jumping site.

Just like high wire bungee, bridge bungee jumping is a thrilling and slightly frightening sport. Therefore, jumping is sometimes a little difficult for people because they're so high up. As one person watching the jumpers says with a smile, 'I think it's great – if someone else is doing it!'

[1]**birthplace:** place where sb or sth was born or started
[2]**commercial:** used for making money

Back at the Nevis jump site, a young woman named Marlene is finding out that it really isn't always easy to jump. She's very nervous and she's having difficulty getting out of the jump pod. It's easy to understand since the view looks very dangerous and frightening from the top. 'Here we go Marlene,' says the instructor, '**lean forward**;[1] five, four, three, two, one!' Marlene finally jumps, crying out as she falls far below.

According to Henry Van Asch, 'the people who have to really try hard to jump are the ones that **get the most out of it**.'[2] At least that's what some people think. It seems that for Marlene, it's a bit different. When the instructor asks, 'How was that?' after her jump, Marlene replies, 'I'm never bungee jumping again!' It doesn't look like Marlene will be bungee jumping again any time soon. But then, perhaps for some people, jumping once is enough!

---

[1]**lean forward:** move your body forward by bending at the waist
[2]**get the most out of sth:** use a situation to get the best possible result

## What do you think?

1. Do you think bungee jumping is dangerous?

2. Would you like to bungee jump at least once? Why or why not?

3. Which of the sports in this story do you like most?

For most jumpers, at the end of the day, they're very happy that they've done it. 'OK, cheers!' says one jumper, as he **toasts**[1] his friend with a cool drink after their adventure. 'Ah, we **deserve**[2] that,' his friend replies. 'That was a good one!' he adds, referring to the jump.

Here in Queenstown, the land that seems made for adventure, the only big question may be: What will they think of doing next? Whatever it is, you can be sure that someone in 'The Adventure Capital of the World' will be ready to give it a try!

---

[1]**toast:** lift your glass and drink with other people
[2]**deserve:** have earned sth; be worthy of

# After You Read

1. On page 4, the word 'cries' can be replaced by:
   A. tears
   B. calls
   C. shouts
   D. songs

2. Henry thinks that people come to Queenstown to bungee jump because:
   A. it's fun.
   B. the jump pod is small.
   C. it's really dangerous.
   D. the pod is really high up.

3. Both men and women like to bungee:
   A. jumping.
   B. jump.
   C. jumper.
   D. jumped.

4. On page 6, 'them' in the third paragraph refers to:
   A. people who love adventure
   B. New Zealanders
   C. bungee jumpers
   D. adventure sports

5. Which of the following is a good heading for page 8?
   A. New Zealand Adventure Invention
   B. Jetboat Uses New Style Propeller
   C. Spinning Machine
   D. Adventure Seekers Dislike Boat

6. On page 8, the word 'pastime' means:
   A. event
   B. job
   C. hobby
   D. boat

7. How many different types of sport are there in Queenstown?
   **A.** two
   **B.** five
   **C.** eighty
   **D.** sixty

8. On page 12, the writer's purpose is to:
   **A.** introduce a new sport.
   **B.** talk about tired hikers.
   **C.** explain a traditional adventure sport.
   **D.** describe the environment around the city.

9. On page 15, the person on the bridge probably thinks that bungee jumping is:
   **A.** easy.
   **B.** scary.
   **C.** awful.
   **D.** boring.

10. According to Henry, angry people get the most out of bungee jumping.
    **A.** True
    **B.** False

11. In the second paragraph on page 19, who does 'they' refer to?
    **A.** the jumpers
    **B.** the men drinking
    **C.** New Zealanders
    **D.** jetboat owners

12. What happens in Queenstown when a new sport is invented?
    **A.** Everyone tries it immediately.
    **B.** Someone will try it.
    **C.** Tourists try it.
    **D.** No one wants to try it.

# Jetboats

A jetboat is a very special type of boat that can be used in very shallow water. It can be operated in as little as twelve inches of water. A jetboat can also make extremely tight turns. In addition, if the boat has openings on the sides, it can actually move through the water sideways, as well as forwards and backwards.

## The History of the Jetboat

Two people were largely responsible for the development of this amazing machine. An Italian man named Secundo Campini had the idea first. In the 1930s and 1940s, he built and tested several jetboat models. However, it was Sir William Hamilton, a New Zealander, who was responsible for the popular jetboats today. The timeline below gives some of the important steps in the machine's development.

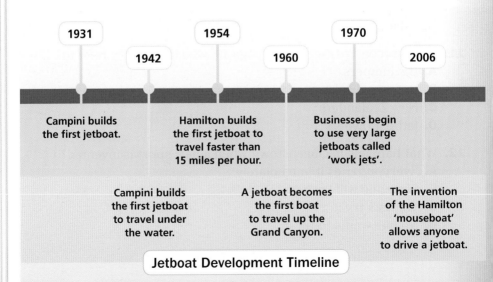

| 1931 | 1942 | 1954 | 1960 | 1970 | 2006 |

Campini builds the first jetboat.

Campini builds the first jetboat to travel under the water.

Hamilton builds the first jetboat to travel faster than 15 miles per hour.

A jetboat becomes the first boat to travel up the Grand Canyon.

Businesses begin to use very large jetboats called 'work jets'.

The invention of the Hamilton 'mouseboat' allows anyone to drive a jetboat.

**Jetboat Development Timeline**

A jetboat can go almost anywhere.

### The Mechanics of a Jetboat

A jetboat does not use a propeller to push itself through the water like other boats. Instead, it takes in water through a large opening under the boat. Then, it pushes the water out of a smaller hole at the back of the boat. This hole is below the level of the water. The action of the water leaving the small hole causes the boat to move forward. Most normal boats have propellers which extend below the bottom of the boat. Many also use a large board, called a 'rudder', to turn right and left. A jetboat, on the other hand, has neither. Instead, jetboat drivers control the direction of the water as it leaves the smaller hole. This is how the driver guides the boat through the water. Because it doesn't have a propeller or rudder, a jetboat can operate in very shallow water and not hit anything below it.

**Word Count:** 345
**Time:** _____

# Words to Know

This story starts in Talkeetna in Alaska, in the United States (U.S.). It ends in an area called Matanuska, near Denali National Park.

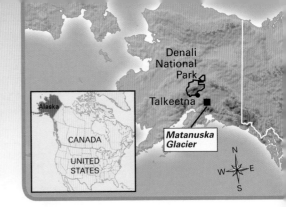

Denali National Park

Talkeetna

Alaska

CANADA

UNITED STATES

Matanuska Glacier

N W E S

**(A)** **In the Mountains.** Here are some activities you can do on a mountain or a glacier. Match the words in the box to the correct picture.

| climbing | hiking | skiing |
|---|---|---|

**1.** _____

**2.** _____

**3.** _____

The Matanuska **Glacier** is over 27 miles long.

**B** **Mountain Weather Conditions.** **Weather** refers to the conditions in the sky and air. Match each weather word to the correct definition.

**1.** cloud: _____

**2.** fine: _____

**3.** fog: _____

**4.** ice: _____

**5.** rain: _____

**6.** snow: _____

**7.** sunshine: _____

**8.** wind: _____

**a.** the light from the sun

**b.** very cold water that has become hard

**c.** a natural, fast movement of air

**d.** white frozen water that falls from the sky in cold weather

**e.** a white or grey mass in the air made from small drops of water

**f.** drops of water falling from the sky

**g.** good or nice

**h.** a heavy grey mass near the ground that makes it difficult to see

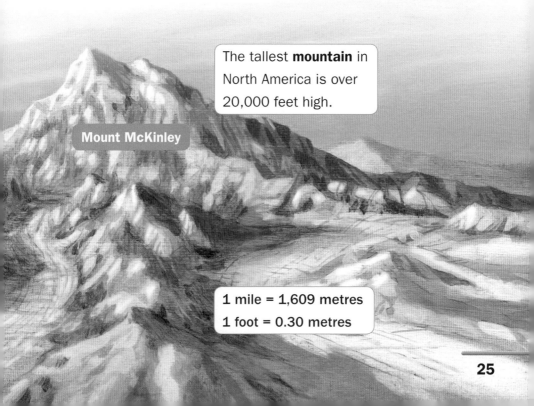

The tallest **mountain** in North America is over 20,000 feet high.

Mount McKinley

1 mile = 1,609 metres

1 foot = 0.30 metres

There's only one thing that's certain about the weather in Alaska – it changes all the time! Sometimes there's rain, sometimes there's wind, and sometimes there's snow. Sometimes the weather is just fine with lots of sunshine.

On one particular day, there's rain and fog all the way from Denali National Park to the town of Talkeetna. There, a group of visitors is planning to fly onto a glacier. They then want to ski down the glacier. But the weather has other plans …

The group really wants to get to the glacier to **ski**.[1] 'So, can we go today?' one of them asks. But the answer is not a good one. 'Uh, not until the **pilots**[2] are **comfortable with**[3] the weather,' replies their **guide**[4] Colby Coombs. He then explains that the clouds are too low, so the group cannot fly. It's too unsafe.

Colby Coombs and Caitlin Palmer are both experienced mountain guides. They run a climbing school. They teach beginner climbers and help experienced climbers to reach the top of Denali. Denali is a mountain that is also known as Mount McKinley. It's the highest mountain in North America.

[1]**ski:** slide over snow as a sport
[2]**pilot:** a person who operates an aeroplane
[3]**comfortable with sth:** accept sth or like it
[4]**guide:** a person whose job is showing places to visitors

Colby and Caitlin are both very good climbers. They're not usually **doubtful**[1] when they're in the mountains. But even they won't take a small plane out in bad weather. 'It's kind of **ornery**[2] weather,' says Colby. 'You usually have to **factor in**[3] a day or two to **put up with**[4] bad weather.'

So, Colby and Caitlin decide on another plan. Instead of taking the group to ski down a **glacier**,[5] they will take them to climb up one. They plan to take the group to a glacier that they can drive to in the car: the Matanuska Glacier.

---

[1]**doubtful:** not sure
[2]**ornery:** bad
[3]**factor in:** include
[4]**put up with:** take into consideration; allow for
[5]**glacier:** a very large mass of ice that moves very slowly

Matanuska is a very big glacier – it's 27 miles long and two miles wide. The name 'Matanuska' comes from an old Russian word for the **Athabascan Indians**[1] who live in the area. The glacier is in a low area that has many trees around it. It formed 2,000 years ago, but it's always moving and changing. It's also always difficult to climb.

[1]**Athabascan Indians:** a group of native people who live in Alaska

The group gets ready to climb one of the Matanuska Glacier's **formations**[1] – a 30-foot wall of ice. At the **base**[2] of the wall, Caitlin explains how to climb it, and it's not going to be easy. 'The most **stable**[3] you're going to be is when you have all the points of your **crampons**[4] sticking on the ice,' says Caitlin.

Caitlin then suggests ways to use crampons. They can help people climb up ice securely and safely. 'Front points in … **heels**[5] down,' she says. 'And if you're going to place a tool,' she adds, '[place it] really solid[ly].'

---

[1]**formation:** sth that has been shaped or formed
[2]**base:** the bottom part of sth
[3]**stable:** strong; secure
[4]**crampon:** a type of climbing tool for ice or snow that fits on the shoe
[5]**heel:** the rounded back part of the foot

tool

wall of ice

heels

front points

crampon

**Part 2** The hike across Matanuska is beautiful, but it can also be very dangerous. One summer, a young man fell into an opening in the ice called a **cirque**,[1] and died.

There are also stories of beginner hikers who get lost and almost die from the cold. In addition, there are **crevasses**[2] everywhere. The climbers have to be careful; they could easily fall in. If they fall into a crevasse, it will be very difficult to get out. Perhaps it will be impossible.

---

[1] **cirque:**  a round opening in the ice
[2] **crevasse:**  a long deep opening in the thick ice of a glacier

The group walks slowly and carefully across the glacier. It's very cold; they have to keep moving to stay warm. Finally, they reach solid ice. They're at **the heart of**[1] the glacier at last.

At this point, the climbers have a wonderful view. They can see a glacial lake with many **seracs**[2] in the background. Seracs are large pieces of blue glacial ice that **stick up**[3] in the air. The glacier creates these seracs as it slowly moves.

Colby explains that an area with many seracs is called an 'ice fall'. He also adds that the seracs can make the area unsafe. This is because they are very big and may fall. He says that a good climber would not hike below an ice fall. It's just not safe.

---

[1]**the heart of:** the centre of
[2]**serac:** a large piece of glacial ice
[3]**stick up:** continue upwards further than sth

crevasse

seracs

glacial lake

cirque

The group enjoys climbing the glacier. It's hard work, but Colby and Caitlin make it look easy. It's a very special feeling when the members of the group reach the top of another ice wall. 'OK, I **made it!**'[1] says one of the beginner climbers happily.

Alaska is home to a large number of glaciers, about 100,000 in total. The people in this group can now say that they have successfully climbed one of them – Matanuska. Now, they only have 99,999 more glaciers to climb!

---

[1]**make it:** succeed in a particular activity

## What do you think?

1. Would you like to climb a glacier?

2. Why or why not?

3. Imagine you are going to climb a glacier.
   What three things will you take with you?

# After You Read

1.  In Alaska there is usually:
    **A.** rain.
    **B.** snow.
    **C.** fog.
    **D.** all of the above

2.  On page 26, the word 'it' in the first paragraph refers to:
    **A.** the village of Talkeetna
    **B.** the weather
    **C.** Alaska
    **D.** Denali National Park

3.  What is another name for Denali?
    **A.** Mount McKinley
    **B.** Athabasca
    **C.** Alaska
    **D.** Talkeetna

4.  The group decides to drive to another glacier because the weather is too dangerous to fly.
    **A.** True
    **B.** False

5.  Which of the following is a good heading for page 33?
    **A.** Large Glaciers
    **B.** Low Area Without Trees
    **C.** All about Matanuska
    **D.** A 2,000-year-old Tree

6.  Which of the following is true about Matanuska?
    **A.** There are only a few trees in the low area.
    **B.** The glacier's name comes from an old Russian word.
    **C.** The glacier is 3 miles wide and 27 miles long.
    **D.** The glacier never changes.

7. On page 34, what does the word 'explains' mean?
   A. decides to do something
   B. believes in something
   C. thinks about something
   D. gives information about

8. Which of the following is safe on a glacier?
   A. a crevasse
   B. a cirque
   C. a crampon
   D. a serac

9. What does Colby think about an area with a lot of seracs?
   A. A good climber will not hike there.
   B. A good climber can hike there.
   C. A good climber will stop and rest there.
   D. A good climber should climb there.

10. On page 40, the word 'special' can be replaced by:
    A. common
    B. wonderful
    C. worrying
    D. interesting

11. In this story, people _____ across and _____ up a glacier.
    A. drive, fly
    B. fly, ski
    C. hike, climb
    D. ski, drive

# ④ICE CLIMBING FOR
# BEGINNERS

Ice climbing is similar to mountain climbing. However, instead of being on hard stone, ice climbers move up, down, and even across walls of cold, glassy ice. There are two types of ice climbing. The first type involves climbing over ice and hard snow on the side of a mountain or glacier. The second type involves climbing up water that has become ice – for example a frozen waterfall. Climbers say that both can be difficult and that both require very serious attention.

**A Frozen Waterfall**

ice axe

boots

**Ice climbers need good boots, strong ropes, and an ice axe.**

rope

One difficult thing about ice climbing is that the ice in one place can change from day to day. It can even change from hour to hour. The best way to go up a wall of ice in the morning may not be the best way to come down again later. Ice climbers have to learn how to see differences in the ice. They must also be able to change their plans accordingly.

Three things are very important to help keep ice climbers safe when they climb. First of all, they need special boots to keep their feet warm. These boots also help to stop them from falling when they put their feet down on the ice. Secondly, ice climbers need an ice axe. They can use this axe to make small openings in the ice. They can then carefully place their feet in the openings. The third important thing they need is a rope system. Climbers often only use one rope, but sometimes they use two.

Now let's take a look at something special that all ice climbers put on their boots – crampons. Crampons hold climbers' feet securely as they place them on the ice. The crampons actually go into the ice and give the climber a secure place to step. People say that crampons are responsible for saving many climbers' lives because they stop them from falling.

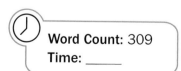

**Word Count: 309**
**Time: _____**

# Words to Know

This story is set in the United States (U.S.). It happens in the Columbia River Gorge, in the states of Oregon and Washington.

**A** **Water Sports.** Read the paragraph. Then write the number of the correct underlined word next to each item in the picture.

Water sports are usually very fast and fun. In water-skiing **(1)**, a person stands on one or two thin skis and a very fast boat **(2)** pulls the skier over the water. In wakeboarding **(3)**, a person stands on a special wide board and a boat pulls them across the water. In kiteboarding **(4)**, a person stands on the same kind of board, but a large kite pulls them. All of these activities can be very enjoyable – especially if the waves **(5)** on the water are big.

kite

Water Sports

board

**B** **An Unusual Inventor.** Read the paragraph. Then match each word with the correct definition.

This story is about water sports in the Columbia River Gorge. A gorge is an area between two mountains, so there is usually a lot of wind there. Cory Roeseler lives in the area, and he loves new things and adventure. Roeseler is a mechanical engineer who likes to invent new things. He likes to design new sports equipment that uses the power of the wind.

**1.** gorge _____

**2.** wind _____

**3.** adventure _____

**4.** mechanical engineer _____

**5.** invent _____

**6.** design _____

**7.** equipment _____

**a.** a narrow place between two high areas

**b.** unusual, exciting experience

**c.** a natural, fast movement of air

**d.** someone who designs and builds machines

**e.** make or draw plans for something

**f.** things used for a particular activity or purpose

**g.** create something that has never been made before

skis

It's a cold winter's day in the Columbia River Gorge. '[I] can't believe what blue sky we've got today! It's beautiful,' says Cory Roeseler as he prepares his **equipment**.[1] It may not be warm, but for Roeseler, the wind makes it a perfect day.

To most people, the very cold wind would feel uncomfortable. However, it gives Roeseler a different feeling. He says, '[It] feels like power … feel some wind!' He then adds, 'It's going to be good today.' But good for what? Roeseler puts on a special **suit**[2] for water sports. He then starts to carry a big kite down to the water. 'OK, let's go **sailing**,'[3] he says with a smile.

---

[1] **equipment:** the tools you need for a particular activity
[2] **suit:** a type of clothing you wear for a particular activity
[3] **sail:** move across water using the power of the wind, usually with a cloth called a 'sail'

You see, Cory Roeseler doesn't just fly kites on windy winter days. Roeseler flies with them! Thirty-year-old Roeseler was one of the first people to really experience the sport of **kiteboarding**.[1] He uses a kite to catch the power of the wind. This wind power has helped Roeseler to do new and interesting things. It's been especially helpful in developing new adventure sports, like kiteboarding.

But what is kiteboarding like? How does it feel? According to Roeseler, 'It's sort of a **rolly**,[2] **wavy**,[3] free feeling … where you know at any moment, you can just **launch**[4] off the water for a few seconds and fly.'

---

[1] **kiteboarding:** the sport of using a large kite to pull a person riding on a board on the water
[2] **rolly:** *(slang)* move from side to side because of wind or waves
[3] **wavy:** *(slang)* move up and down because of wind or waves
[4] **launch:** go up into the air quickly

And that's exactly what Roeseler does. As the kite pulls him quickly along, he lifts himself out of the water and launches into the air. That may be why the young **mechanical engineer**[1] compares kiteboarding to the way birds fly. He says that the power of the wind in a kite can be like a bird moving its **wings**.[2] The lifting power, or 'lift', of both things can **overcome gravity**.[3] This lift allows them both to 'fly'.

---

[1] **mechanical engineer:** sb who designs and builds machines
[2] **wing:** part of a bird's body that is moved to fly
[3] **overcome gravity:** become stronger than the natural force that pulls things to Earth

The power of the wind in a kite
is like the lift of a bird's wings.

Wind power is something that's easily found in the **gorge**[1] which divides Washington and Oregon. That makes the Columbia River Gorge one of the best places in the world to kiteboard. However, for inventor Cory Roeseler, the gorge is more than just a place to have fun; it's a place where he can test his new inventions.

Roeseler has always loved water sports. When he was a teenager, he was the first person to 'test pilot', or try out, the sport of kite-skiing. Usually, people water-ski behind a boat. However, Roeseler decided to use wind power to ski behind a kite. It worked. Later, he became a mechanical engineer. Then, in the 1990s, he invented and designed a lot of water sports equipment. Eventually, he became famous in the area of water sports.

---

[1]**gorge:** a deep valley where a river has cut through rock

## Sequence the Events

**What is the correct order of the events? Write numbers.**

_____ invented water sports equipment

_____ became famous

_____ was a test pilot for kite-skiing

_____ became a mechanical engineer

Now, Roeseler is ready to test his newest invention for playing with the wind. To do this, Roeseler has asked his friends for some help. He takes the group to the water to show them his invention. It's a new kind of **wakeboarding**[1] boat that has a sail on the back. Roeseler explains how the sail works. 'The sail's going to **stabilise**[2] us so we don't **tip over**,'[3] he says excitedly.

However, his friends don't seem as certain. Roeseler's friend Jeff, who will be testing the invention, is watching **nervously**[4] nearby. 'Why are you nervous?' someone asks. 'I've never seen anything else like that before,' he says, laughing. 'So it's a little **freaky**,'[5] he explains. But what makes Roeseler's boat so different?

---

[1]**wakeboarding:** the sport of being pulled behind a boat while riding on a short, wide board on the water
[2]**stabilise:** keep in place; stop sudden changes
[3]**tip over:** fall to the side
[4]**nervous:** worried about a future event
[5]**freaky:** unusual in an unpleasant or unexpected way

In recent years, more and more people have started using towers for wakeboarding. A tower is a structure that is put on a wakeboarding boat. It allows people to place the wakeboarding rope higher. This higher rope gives more lift to the wakeboarder and makes it easier to jump in the air. It's also easier on the wakeboarder's body.

Roeseler's design is similar to that of other wakeboarding boats. However, his tower is 17 feet above the water. That's six feet higher than other wakeboarding boats. The higher rope will allow the wakeboarder to jump even higher than before! Roeseler has also added a sail to the tower. The sail will stabilise the tower and the wakeboarder when the boat is moving.

1 foot = 0.31 metres

wakeboarding rope

tower

sail

**Roeseler's New Invention**

Jeff jumps into the water and the boat starts to move. As the boat goes faster, he is able to stand up on his wakeboard. He then starts moving quickly and easily across the water. After a few moments, he speeds up, goes towards a wave, and launches high into the air. The new invention works! Everyone is very happy. 'Nice!' says Jeff as he gets back in the boat. 'It works,' he says with surprise. 'It's **nuts**.[1] I didn't think it would.'

And how does Roeseler feel about the **apparent**[2] success of his invention? 'I'm a little more **confident**[3] ... but, we'll see. It's got to go on a big wakeboard boat and get tested in the right **environment**,'[4] he explains.

---

[1]**nuts:** crazy or not normal; not expected
[2]**apparent:** when sth seems to be true
[3]**confident:** certain of one's abilities
[4]**environment:** the conditions in which people carry on a particular activity

For Cory Roeseler, the right environment seems to be the Columbia River Gorge. For him, it's the right place to live, and the right place to find adventure with his new water sports.

According to Roeseler, life sometimes seems almost **too good to be true**.[1] For him and his friends, living in the area is so wonderful that it's like being in a dream. He adds that they're also happy that they're not going to wake up and find that it's gone. It seems like Roeseler and his friends want every day to be a water sports adventure.

---

[1]**too good to be true:** so good that you cannot believe that such a situation is possible

## Infer Meaning

1. How does Cory Roeseler feel about the Columbia River Gorge?

2. What does he mean by 'it's like being in a dream'?

# After You Read

1. On page 48, how does Cory Roeseler feel about the wind?
   A. uncomfortable
   B. happy
   C. unsure
   D. nervous

2. On page 51, the word 'experience' in the first paragraph means:
   A. fly
   B. use
   C. do
   D. be

3. How does the kite help Roeseler?
   A. Its power lifts him.
   B. He uses it to sail better.
   C. It keeps him warm.
   D. It reduces his speed.

4. Kiteboarding feels _____ flying.
   A. just
   B. about
   C. way
   D. like

5. Which is a good heading for the first paragraph on page 54?
   A. Inventor Dislikes Columbia Gorge
   B. Impossible to Kiteboard in Gorge
   C. New Sport at Columbia Gorge
   D. Not Enough Wind At Gorge

6. When Roeseler started kite-skiing, he was:
   A. under ten years old.
   B. aged between 13 and 19.
   C. 12 years old.
   D. thirty years old.

7. On page 54, 'it's' in the first paragraph refers to:
   A. the gorge
   B. the kiteboard
   C. a place
   D. the wind

8. According to page 56, what do Roeseler's friends think about the wakeboarding boat?
   A. They think it's great.
   B. They think it will definitely work.
   C. They are not sure about it.
   D. They really dislike it.

9. Roeseler's wakeboard boat is different because it has a small tower.
   A. True
   B. False

10. On page 58, the word 'allow' in the second paragraph means:
    A. give
    B. let
    C. make
    D. agree

11. Roeseler thinks his latest invention:
    A. needs more testing.
    B. is nuts.
    C. is unbelievable.
    D. works perfectly.

12. According to page 62, why is every day a good day for Roeseler?
    A. He can dream about kiteboarding.
    B. He loves where he lives and what he does.
    C. The weather is always good in the gorge.
    D. all of the above

# My Water-Skiing
## ⑥ Adventure

### 12th June

Well, this is it ... I'm taking my first water-skiing lesson tomorrow morning. I'm a little nervous, but it'll be an adventure!

### 13th June

I met my teacher early this morning. Before we started, he said I had to practise on dry land. First, he asked me to sit down on the ground. Then he gave me the 'tow rope', the line that will connect me to the boat. While he held the rope, I had to stand up only using the power in my legs. It wasn't easy. I'm just not used to doing that! He also told me to remember one important thing – I must drop the tow rope immediately if I fall over.

Then the fun really began. We put the equipment into the boat and went out into deep water. My teacher said that he would start the boat slowly and then go faster. My job was to stand up when the boat was going quickly. It sounded easy. But as soon as I stood up, I tipped over. Then, I forgot to drop the rope! I went flying through the water and my skis came off. I felt really silly and we had to start again. I tried this 25 times, but I could not stand up. Water-skiing is harder than I expected.

**Water-skiing is hard work but fun!**

### 14th June

Today things were a little better. After five attempts, I was able to stand up. I waited until I found my balance on the skis, and then stood up slowly. I was surprised at how hard the water felt under the skis. It was like stone. The wind on my face was really strong. I was water-skiing and it felt wonderful!

### 15th June

Today was even better than yesterday! There were some big waves and I learned how to move over a wave without falling. Tomorrow I'm going to try it using only one ski – I can't wait!

 **Word Count:** 325
**Time:** _____

## Grammar Focus: Gerund Subjects

- Gerunds can be used as the subject of a sentence:
  _Hiking is very good exercise._
  _Bungee jumping is a new adventure sport._

  A gerund is the _–ing_ form of the verb, used as a noun: _jump  jumping_

### Spelling Rules

- If the verb ends in _–e_, drop the _–e_ and add _–ing_: _live  living_

- If the verb has only one syllable and ends in consonant-vowel-consonant, double the last consonant and add _–ing_: _sit  sitting_

- If the verb has two syllables that end in consonant-vowel-consonant, double the last consonant and add _–ing_: _begin  beginning_

- If the verb ends in _–ie_, change the _–ie_ to _–y_ and add _–ing_: _die  dying_

## Grammar Practice: Gerund Subjects
Complete each sentences with the gerund form of a word from the box.

| cook | drink | ~~send~~ | talk | ski | listen |
|------|-------|----------|------|-----|--------|

**e.g.** _Sending_____ an email is much faster than sending a letter.

1. _____ dinner takes me about an hour every night.

2. _____ on your mobile phone while you are driving is very dangerous.

3. _____ coffee at night is a bad idea. You won't sleep well.

4. _____ to music is a good way to relax.

5. _____ is a very popular sport in cold countries.

## Grammar Focus: Present Perfect Questions with Adverbs of Frequency

■ In present perfect questions with *never*, students may be confused about how to answer, similar to negative questions such as *Haven't you ever...?* Explain that the answer is *yes* if the person has done the action and *no* if the person has not. For example: *Have you never eaten fish?* If the person has eaten fish, she answers: *Yes, I have.*

| Have | you we they | always ever never | taken the train to school? eaten dinner at 7:00? finished the homework? been to France? | Yes, I have. No, I haven't. |
|------|-------------|-------------------|-----------------------------------------------------------------------------------------|-----------------------------|
| Has | he she | | | Yes, he has. No, he hasn't. |

## Grammar Practice: Present Perfect Questions

Write questions with the present perfect tense and frequency adverbs. They will give *yes* or *no* answers.

**e.g.** you/always/come to class on time
  *Have you always come to class on time? (Yes, I have OR No, I haven't).*

1. your friends/always/tell you the truth

   _____

2. the teacher/ever/give us tests

   _____

3. we/never/make a mistake

   _____

## Grammar Focus: Present Perfect with Adverbs of Frequency

■ The present perfect is formed by the auxiliary *have/has* + past participle. When the present perfect is used with frequency adverbs: 1) the adverb goes between the auxiliary and the main verb; 2) it refers to an action that has (or hasn't) happened sometime before now or to a repeated past action.

| | | | |
|---|---|---|---|
| I, You, We, They | (have/haven't) | always | enjoyed reading. |
| She, He, (It) | has/hasn't | | done my homework on time. |

| | | |
|---|---|---|
| I, You, We, They | have never ('ve never) | |
| | haven't ever | come to class late. |
| | | flown in an airplane. |
| She, He, (It) | has never ('s never) | |
| | hasn't ever | |

## Grammar Practice: Present Perfect with Adverbs of Frequency

Write true sentences about yourself. Use *always* and *never.*

**e.g.** *I have always walked to school.*

1. _____

2. _____

3. _____

4. _____

5. _____

## Grammar Focus: Superlative Adjectives

■ Use superlative adjectives to compare groups of things (3 or more).

| Type of adjective | Simple form | Superlative |
|---|---|---|
| one syllable | tall | the tallest |
| one syllable ending in –e<br>add –st | large | the largest |
| ending in consonant + vowel +<br>consonant<br>double the consonant and add<br>–est | big | the biggest |
| ending in –y<br>change –y to –i and add –est | easy | the easiest |
| two or more syllables | modern | the most modern |
| irregular | good | the best |
|  | bad | the worst |
|  | far | the farthest |

## Grammar Practice: Superlative Adjectives

Write sentences about these things with superlative adjectives.

**e.g.** Mt. Everest/mountain/high/world

_Mt. Everest is the highest mountain in the world._

1. Tokyo/city/large/Japan

2. 'Mona Lisa'/painting/expensive/France

_____

3. Amazon/river/long/Brazil

_____

4. Antarctica/cold/place/Earth

_____

## Video Practice

**A.** Watch Part 1 of the video of *The Adventure Capital of the World* and circle the word you hear.

1. 'People come from around the world to (do/try) adventure sports in Queenstown...'
2. 'There are many people (hoping/waiting) for a chance to do it.'
3. 'If you like exciting adventure sports, New Zealand is the (place/country) to do them.'
4. 'In New Zealand, it seems that nearly every day someone (designs/creates) another adventure sport.'

**B.** Watch Part 2 of the video and write down the word you hear.

1. 'One of the newest _____ involves a five-hour hike up a mountain.'
2. 'The helicopter turns the five-hour hike into a five-minute flight back to the _____!'
3. 'Maybe for some people, jumping once is _____.'
4. 'Most jumpers are _____ that they did it.'

**C.** Watch the entire video of *Alaskan Ice Climbing* and find the main idea.

    **a.** Many visitors like to go to Alaska for outdoor vacations.

    **b.** The weather in Alaska is very cold most of the year.

    **c.** On a sports vacation in Alaska, you must be careful.

**D.** Watch Part 1 of the video again and fill in the numbers in the sentence.

    **1.** 'Matanuska is a very big glacier. It's _____ miles long and _____ miles wide.'

    **2.** 'It formed _____ years ago, but it's always changing.'

    **3.** 'The group gets ready to climb one of Matanuska's formations, a _____ -foot wall of ice.'

**E.** Watch Part 2 of the video again and circle the word you hear.

    **1.** 'The hike across Matanuska is (beautiful/wonderful).'

    **2.** 'The climbers have to be careful; they could easily fall (off/in).'

    **3.** 'Finally, they reach solid ice – the (centre/heart) of the glacier.'

    **4.** 'He also adds that they can make the area (dangerous/unsafe).'

    **5.** 'It's hard work, but Colby and Caitlin make it look (easy/fun).'

    **6.** 'Alaska is home to 100,000 glaciers. These (visitors/people) can say they have climbed one – Matanuska.'

**F.** Watch the video of *Water Sports Adventure* and take notes on the sports equipment you see.

_____

_____

_____

**G.** Read the sentences. Watch the video and circle the word you hear.
1. 'To most people, the very cold wind would feel (uncomfortable/comfortable).'
2. 'Thirty-year-old Roeseler was one of the first people to really experience the sport of (kiteboarding/wakeboarding).'
3. 'Later, he became a mechanical (engine/engineer).'
4. 'It's one of the best (areas/places) in the world to kiteboard.'
5. 'In the 1990s, he (invented/tried) and designed a lot of water sports equipment.'

**H.** Watch the video again and take notes to use when you answer the questions. Then write complete sentences.

1. Why is Roeseler's friend nervous about the wakeboarding boat?

_____

2. Why do wakeboarders prefer a higher rope?

_____

3. Why has Roeseler added a sail to the boat's tower?

_____

4. What is the last thing Roeseler talks about on the video?

_____

(1) There are other activities for tourists to do in New Zealand in addition to bungee jumping. (2) Jetboat rides are very popular with tourists. (3) These boats are also especially useful in New Zealand where the rivers are shallow. (4) Jetboats do not have any propellers so they can turn around very quickly in a small space. (5) The drivers like to do this to give their passengers a thrill. (6) A slower pastime, but also very popular, is hiking in the mountains. (7) However, New Zealanders have added something special to this activity. (8) Guides lead hikers on a five-hour walk up a mountain. (9) When they get to the top, they look at the view for 10 minutes. (10) Then a helicopter takes them on a five-minute ride back to the city!

1. Jetboats _____.
   A. are very exciting to travel in
   B. were originally made to use in the ocean
   C. usually move quite slowly
   D. are sometimes used by fisherman

2. The word 'they' in sentence 4 refers to _____.
   A. propellers
   B. tourists
   C. jetboats
   D. jetboat drivers

3. Where does this sentence go?
   This means that they can complete the hike in half the time.
   A. after sentence 4
   B. after sentence 6
   C. after sentence 7
   D. after sentence 10

4. A _____ can fly above the ground.
   A. bridge
   B. helicopter
   C. jetboat
   D. hike

5. The word 'shallow' means the opposite of _____.
   A. wide
   B. fast
   C. deep
   D. tall

6. _____ in a jetboat is a lot of fun.
   A. Ride
   B. Riding
   C. Ridden
   D. Rode

7. If you're tired after climbing the mountain, _____ the helicopter back is a good idea.
   A. take
   B. taken
   C. taking
   D. took

8. How long do mountain climbers stay at the top of the mountain?
   _____
   A. five minutes
   B. two minutes
   C. one hour
   D. 10 minutes

(1) Many visitors come to Alaska to ski. (2) When they can't ski down a glacier, the visitors make other plans. (3) Today, they decide to climb up a glacier. (4) They choose the Matanuska Glacier in Denali National Park. (5) It is very large – about 27 miles long and two miles wide. (6) It's over 2,000 years old and it's always changing. (7) The walls of the glacier are 30 feet tall. (8) It is beautiful on top of the glacier, but it can be unsafe. (9) Sometimes people die when they fall into an opening. (10) The group climbs the glacier. (11) It isn't easy and they feel very happy when they finish.

9. How tall is the Matanuska Glacier?
   A. 27 miles
   B. 2,000 feet
   C. two miles
   D. 30 feet

10. The Matanuska Glacier _____.
    A. is in Denali National Park
    B. is a small glacier
    C. never changes
    D. is very safe

11. Where should this sentence go?
    One summer a man died on Matanuska Glacier.
    A. after sentence 5
    B. after sentence 8
    C. after sentence 9
    D. after sentence 10

12. What is the best title for this paragraph?
    A. An Unsafe Climb
    B. Climbing the Matanuska Glacier
    C. Skiing Down a Glacier
    D. A Small Glacier

**13.** The word 'it' in sentence 5 refers to _____.
   **A.** The Matanuska Glacier
   **B.** Denali National Park
   **C.** The top of the Matanuska Glacier
   **D.** The wall of the Matanuska Glacier

**14.** The Matanuska Glacier is _____ miles long.
   **A.** two
   **B.** ten
   **C.** 27
   **D.** 30

**15.** Which of the following means 'very cold water that has become hard'?
   **A.** rain
   **B.** wind
   **C.** fog
   **D.** ice

**16.** Snow is _____.
   **A.** the light from the sun
   **B.** a heavy gray mass near the ground
   **C.** white frozen water that falls from the sky
   **D.** a natural fast movement of air

**17.** Colby and Caitlin are _____ climbers in the group.
   **A.** experience
   **B.** most experienced
   **C.** the experiencedest
   **D.** the most experienced

**18.** The Bering Glacier is _____ glacier in Alaska.
   **A.** the longer
   **B.** longest
   **C.** the longest
   **D.** the most long

(1) Cory Roeseler is a mechanical engineer who likes to invent things. (2) He invented kiteboarding in the 1990s. (3) He also designed a lot of kiteboarding equipment around the same time. (4) Wakeboarding is a water sport which involves using a special wide board pulled behind a boat. (5) Now Roeseler has designed something to make wakeboarding more enjoyable and easier. (6) It involves putting a 17-foot tower on the back of a wakeboarding boat. (7) This allows the wakeboarder to jump high up in the air. (8) It is also easier on the wakeboarder's body. (9) Roeseler's friend, Jeff, is getting ready to test the new equipment. (10) He is a little worried. (11) 'I've never seen anything like that before.' (12) But he jumps in the water and soon he is able to stand up. (13) When Jeff gets back in the boat he says, 'I didn't think it would work, but it did!' (14) So it's one more success for Cory Roeseler – sportsman, engineer, and inventor.

19. Where did Roeseler put the tower?
   A. in the water
   B. on the right side of the boat
   C. on the back of the boat
   D. on land

20. The word 'it' in sentence 14 refers to _____.
   A. the wakeboarding boat
   B. Roeseler's kiteboard
   C. Roeseler's latest invention
   D. a wave

21. The writer thinks that _____.
   A. Roeseler is a very special man
   B. wakeboarding is not enjoyable
   C. Jeff is a great engineer
   D. the tower may not be safe

22. A good heading for this paragraph is _____.
   A. Roeseler's First Invention
   B. Cory and Jeff
   C. Another Success for Roeseler
   D. Kiteboarding USA

23. Where should this sentence go? Then he begins to move quickly and easily across the water.
   A. after sentence 3
   B. after sentence 5
   C. after sentence 7
   D. after sentence 12

**24.** What did Jeff think about the new equipment before he tested it?
   **A.** He was sure it would work perfectly.
   **B.** He thought it looked like a normal piece of equipment.
   **C.** He thought Roeseler should test it himself.
   **D.** He was not sure it would work well.

**25.** Someone who studies how machines work is _____.
   **A.** an adventurer
   **B.** a wakeboarder
   **C.** a boater
   **D.** a mechanical engineer

**26.** A natural fast movement of air is _____.
   **A.** waves
   **B.** wind
   **C.** a gorge
   **D.** an invention

**27.** Roeseler's friend, Jeff, _____ him test new equipment.
   **A.** has helped often
   **B.** has helped sometimes
   **C.** has often helped
   **D.** helped sometimes has

**28.** Roeseler's inventions _____ successful.
   **A.** have usually been
   **B.** alway have been
   **C.** have been usually
   **D.** have been always

# Key 答案

## The Adventure Capital of the World
**Words to Know: A. 1.** c **2.** e **3.** f **4.** b **5.** d **6.** a  **B. 1.** jetboat **2.** thrill
**3.** propeller **4.** shallow **5.** frightening
**Scan for Information: 1.** five hours **2.** 10 or 15 minutes **3.** in a helicopter
**4.** five minutes
**What do you think?:** open answers
**After You Read: 1.** C **2.** D **3.** B **4.** D **5.** A **6.** C **7.** D **8.** A **9.** B **10.** B **11.** C
**12.** B

## Alaskan Ice Climbing
**Words to Know: A. 1.** skiing **2.** hiking **3.** climbing **B. 1.** e **2.** g **3.** h **4.** b
**5.** f **6.** d **7.** a **8.** c
**Infer Meaning:** they – Colby and Caitlin; them – the group; one – glacier
**What do you think?:** open answers
**After You Read: 1.** D **2.** B **3.** A **4.** A **5.** C **6.** B **7.** D **8.** C **9.** A **10.** B **11.** C

## Water Sports Adventure
**Words to Know: A.** (From left to right) **3.** (wakeboarding)
**4.** (kiteboarding) **2.** (boat) **5.** (waves) **1.** (water-skiing)
**B. 1.** a **2.** c **3.** b **4.** d **5.** g **6.** e **7.** f
**Sequence the Events:** 3, 4, 1, 2
**Infer Meaning:** (suggested answers) **1.** He thinks it's the right place to live
and do water sports. **2.** He means it's too good to be true.
**After You Read: 1.** B **2.** C **3.** A **4.** D **5.** C **6.** B **7.** A **8.** C **9.** B **10.** B **11.** A
**12.** B

## Grammar Practice

**Gerund Subjects: 1.** Cooking **2.** Talking **3.** Drinking **4.** Listening **5.** Skiing

**Present Perfect Questions: 1.** Have your friends always told you the truth? **2.** Has the teacher ever given us tests? **3.** Have we never made a mistake?

**Present Perfect with Adverbs of Frequency:** open answers

**Superlative Adjectives: 1.** Tokyo is the largest city in Japan. **2.** The 'Mona Lisa' is the most expensive painting in France. **3.** The Amazon is the longest river in Brazil. **4.** Antarctica is the coldest place on Earth.

## Video Practice

**A. 1.** do **2.** waiting **3.** place **4.** creates **B. 1.** adventures **2.** city **3.** enough **4.** happy **C.** c **D. 1.** 27; two **2.** 2,000 **3.** 30 **E. 1.** beautiful **2.** in **3.** heart **4.** unsafe **5.** easy **6.** people **F.** (open answer) **G. 1.** uncomfortable **2.** kiteboarding **3.** engineer **4.** places **5.** invented **H. 1.** The sail is a new idea; he's never seen anything similar. **2.** It's easier to jump in the air, and it's easier on their bodies. **3.** The sail will stabilise the tower and keep the boat from tipping over. **4.** He talks about testing his invention on a bigger boat.

## Exit Test

**1.** A **2.** C **3.** D **4.** B **5.** C **6.** B **7.** C **8.** D **9.** D **10.** A **11.** C **12.** B **13.** A **14.** C **15.** D **16.** C **17.** D **18.** C **19.** C **20.** C **21.** A **22.** C **23.** D **24.** D **25.** D **26.** B **27.** C **28.** A

# English - Chinese Vocabulary List 中英對照生詞表

(Arranged in alphabetical order)

| | | | |
|---|---|---|---|
| apparent | 明顯的 | lean forward | 身體向前傾 |
| Athabascan Indians | 阿拉斯加原住民 | make it | 成功做到某事 |
| base | 底部 | mechanical engineer | 機械工程 |
| birthplace | 來源，出處 | nervous | 緊張 |
| bring it on | 開始 | nuts | 瘋狂 |
| cirque | 冰斗 | ornery | 壞，不好 |
| comfortable with sth | 接受 | overcome gravity | 反地心吸力 |
| commercial | 商業 | pastime | 消遣 |
| confident | 自信 | phew | 唉 |
| cord | 粗繩 | pilot | 機師 |
| crampon | 防滑鐵釘 | propeller | 螺旋槳 |
| crazy | 神經病 | proud | 引以為傲 |
| crevasse | 冰川裂隙 | put up with | 忍受 |
| deserve | 應得 | rolly | 搖擺不定 |
| doubtful | 懷疑 | sail | 揚帆航行 |
| environment | 環境 | serac | 冰河的大冰塊 |
| equipment | 設備 | ski | 滑雪 |
| factor in | 把 ...計入 | spin on a dime | 急速轉彎 |
| formation | 形狀 | stabilise | 穩住 |
| freaky | 古怪 | stable | 穩定 |
| gap | 空隙 | stick up | 豎起 |
| get the most out of sth | 得到最多益處 | suit | 服裝 |
| glacier | 冰河 | the heart of | 中心 |
| gorge | 峽谷 | thrill | 興奮 |
| guide | 導遊 | tip over | 翻倒 |
| heel | 腳跟 | toast | 乾杯 |
| immediate lifestyle | 冒險的生活方式 | too good to be true | 好得難以置信 |
| invention | 發明 | underside | 底層 |
| jump pod | 跳台 | wakeboarding | 花式滑水 |
| kiteboarding | 滑浪 | wavy | 多浪的 |
| launch | 起飛 | wing | 翅膀 |
| | | work sth out | 計算 |